Mole sets off for the Wild Wood.

Ratty gets ready to rescue Mole.

Mole does his spring cleaning.

Clever Mr. Toad escapes from prison.

Craigiebank Church
Sunday
School

Presented to

CAROLINE HOPE

Beginners' Dept.

Session: 1997/98

CHRISTIAN ART
TEL: 01323 410930

©1991 GRANDREAMS LIMITED

Stories re-told by Anne McKie. Illustrations by Ken McKie.

This edition published 1997.

Published by

GRANDREAMS LIMITED
435–437 Edgware Road, Little Venice, London W2 1TH

Printed in Hungary.

THE WIND IN THE WILLOWS
Collection

The River Bank

The Open Road

The Wild Wood

The Adventures of Mr. Toad

There are lots of stories from
'The Wind in the Willows' about the adventures of the four
friends, Mole, Rat, Toad and Badger.
This story is about how Mole and Ratty met for the first time...
by the river bank.

THE WIND IN THE WILLOWS

The River Bank

The Mole had been working very hard all the morning, spring-cleaning his little room. First with brooms, then with dusters; then on ladders and steps and chairs, with a brush and a bucket of whitewash. There were splashes of paint all over his black fur, his poor back ached and his arms were tired.

Spring was in the air! Mole could feel it, even in the dark depth of his little house underground.

Suddenly, he threw his brush down on the floor. "Bother!" he said. "Oh blow! Hang spring-cleaning!" and bolted out of his house without even waiting to put his coat on.

Once in the steep little tunnel outside his front door, he scrabbled and scratched and scraped, working busily with his little paws and muttering to himself, "Up we go! Up we go!" till at last, pop! his snout came out into the sunlight and he found himself rolling in the warm grass of a great meadow.

"This is fine!" he said to himself. "This is better than whitewashing!"

The warm spring sunshine and the soft breeze made the Mole jump for joy. With the sound of happy bird song in his ears, Mole went on his way across the meadow until he came to a gap in the hedge on the far side.

"Stop!" said an elderly rabbit at the gap. "Sixpence to use our private road!" But he was bowled over by Mole as he trotted by.

On and on through the meadows he wandered, along the hedgerows, across the copses until, suddenly, he stood by the edge of a river.

Never in his life had he seen a river before. It chuckled and gurgled, the water all glints and gleams and sparkles. Mole was bewitched.

He trotted along by the side of the river until he was quite tired out. Then he sat on the bank while the river clattered on.

As he sat on the grass and looked across the river, a dark hole in the bank opposite, just above the water's edge, caught his eye. "What a nice snug house that would make!" thought Mole dreamily.

As he gazed, something bright and small seemed to twinkle in the hole. Then, to his surprise, it winked, and Mole saw it was an eye. Gradually a small face appeared. A brown little face with whiskers, small neat ears and thick silky hair. It was the Water Rat!

Then the two animals stood
and looked at each other.

"Hello, Mole!" said the Water
Rat.

"Hello, Rat!" said the Mole.

"Would you like to come
over?" asked the Rat.

"How can I do that?" said Mole
rather crossly, for he knew nothing at
all about riverside life and its ways.

The Rat said nothing, but stooped down and unfastened a
rope and pulled on it; then stepped into a little blue and white
boat - just the size for two animals.

Then the Rat rowed smartly across the river and tied up.
He held out his paw as the Mole stepped gingerly down. "Lean on
that!" he said. "Now then, step lively!" and the Mole, to his
surprise, found himself actually sitting in a real boat.

"This has been a wonderful day!" said Mole, as the Rat rowed away. "Do you know, I've never been in a boat before in all my life!"

"What?" cried the Rat, open-mouthed. "Never been in a boat - what have you been doing then?"

"Is it so nice as all that?" asked the Mole, shyly. Then he leaned back in his seat and looked at the cushions and the oars, and lots of interesting things as the boat swayed gently under him.

The Water Rat leaned forward on his oar and said solemnly, "Believe me, my young friend, there is nothing - absolutely nothing - half so much worth doing as simply messing about in boats. Simply messing," he went on dreamily, "messing-about-in-boats."

"Look ahead, Rat!" cried Mole suddenly. It was too late. The boat struck the bank at full tilt, and the Rat lay at the bottom of the boat, with his heels in the air.

How the two friends laughed as the Rat picked himself up. "Look here!" said Rat to Mole. "If you've really nothing else to do this morning, why don't we row down the river together, and have a long day of it?"

The Mole waggled his toes from sheer happiness, sighed and leaned back into the soft cushions. "What a day I'm having!" he said. "Let's start at once!"

"Just a minute," said the Rat, as he tied up the boat to a ring on his landing-stage. Then he climbed up into his hole in the river bank. After a short while he came out carrying a very heavy wicker picnic-basket.

"Shove that under your feet," he said to the Mole as he passed it down into the boat.

"What's inside it?" asked the Mole, wriggling with curiosity.

"There's cold chicken inside it," replied the Rat: "Coldtonguecoldhamcoldbeefpickledgherkinssaladfrenchrollscress sandwichespottedmeatgingerbeerlemonadesodawater" -

"Oh stop, stop!" cried the excited Mole. "This is too much!"

"Do you really think so?" asked the Rat seriously. "It's only what I always take on these little river trips."

The Mole never heard a word he was saying, he was far too busy enjoying all the different scents and sounds of the river. As the Water Rat rowed quietly along, Mole dreamily trailed a paw in the water.

After a while, Rat began to tell Mole all about his life by the river. "It's my world, and I don't want any other!"

"But isn't it a bit dull at times?" asked Mole, timidly. "Just you and the river and no one else to talk to?"

"No one else!" the Rat laughed. "There are far too many people sometimes. Otters, kingfishers, dabchicks, moorhens, around and about all day long!"

"What lies over there?" asked Mole, waving his paw towards the dark woodland across the meadow.

"That's the Wild Wood," said Rat. "We don't go there very much, we river bankers."

"Aren't they - very nice people in there?" asked the Mole, nervously.

"Well," replied the Rat, "let me see. The squirrels are all right, but the rabbits are a mixed lot. And then there's Badger, who lives right in the heart of it. Dear old Badger! Nobody interferes with him. They'd better not!"

"Why, who should interfere with him?" asked Mole.

The Rat hesitated, then explained. "There are others. Weasels - and stoats - and foxes - and so on. They're alright in a way - but they break out sometimes, there's no denying it, and then you really can't trust them, and that's the fact."

"And beyond the Wild Wood again?" Mole asked, "where it's all blue and dim, and you can see what may be hills or the smoke of towns, or just clouds?"

"Beyond the Wild Wood comes the Wild World," said the Rat. "And that's something that doesn't matter to you or me. I've never been there and I'm never going, nor you, either, if you've got any sense at all! Now then! Here's our backwater at last, where we're going to have lunch!"

Leaving the main part of the river, they floated through to a little lake. Grassy green banks sloped down on either side. Brown snaky tree-roots gleamed below the surface of the quiet water. Ahead of them the water tumbled over a weir that drove a dripping mill wheel. It was so beautiful that Mole could only hold up both front paws and gasp, "Oh my! Oh my! Oh my!"

The Rat brought the boat alongside the bank, tied her up, helped Mole safely ashore, and lifted out the picnic-basket.

The Mole begged to be allowed to unpack it all by himself. Rat was pleased to let him while he stretched full length on the grass for a rest.

Very excited, Mole shook out the tablecloth and spread it, then he took out all the mysterious packets one by one and arranged their contents in order, still gasping, "Oh my! Oh my!"

When all was ready, the Rat said, "Now pitch in, old fellow!" which Mole gladly did, for he had started his spring-cleaning very early that morning, and it had been a very long time since breakfast.

"What are you looking at?" Rat asked the Mole, when they had had enough to eat, and Mole's eyes were able to wander off the tablecloth a little.

"I am looking," said the Mole, "at a streak of bubbles that I see travelling along the surface of the water. That strikes me as funny!"

"Bubbles? Oho!" said the Rat laughing.

A broad glistening nose showed itself above the edge of the bank, and the Otter hauled himself out and shook the water from his coat.

"Why didn't you invite me?" the Otter asked Rat, as he went towards the food. "All the world seems to be out on the river today!" the Otter went on. "I came up here to try and get a moment's peace, and then I stumble upon you fellows!"

There was a rustle behind them, coming from a thick leafy hedge - suddenly a stripy head appeared.

"Come on, old Badger!" shouted the Rat.

The Badger trotted forward a couple of steps, then grunted, "H'm! company," and turned his back and disappeared from view.

"That's just the sort of fellow he is!" said Rat quite disappointed. "Simply hates company. That's the last we'll see of him today. Well, tell us who's out on the river?" the Water Rat asked Otter.

"Mr. Toad's out," replied the Otter. "In his brand new racing boat; new clothes, new everything!"

The Water Rat smiled. "Once it was sailing, then it was punting, last year it was house-boating. It's always the same, whatever he does he soon gets tired of it, then starts on something fresh!"

From where they sat they could get a glimpse of the main stream of the river; just then a little racing boat flashed by with Mr. Toad rowing. He was short and stout, splashing badly and rolling all over the place. The Rat stood up and shouted to him, but Mr. Toad shook his head and sped on his way.

"He'll be out that boat in a minute if he rolls like that," said the Rat, sitting down.

"Of course he will," chuckled the Otter. "Did I ever tell you that story about Toad and the lock keeper?" Just then a Mayfly swooped low over the water...suddenly it had vanished - and so had the Otter. All that Mole could see of him was a streak of bubbles on the water.

"Well, well," said the Rat. "I suppose we ought to be moving. I wonder which of us had better pack the picnic-basket?"

"Oh, please let me," said the Mole. So, of course, Rat let him.

Packing the basket was not quite so pleasant work as unpacking it. It never is. But the Mole was quite determined to enjoy it. Just when he had got the basket packed and strapped up tightly, he saw a plate staring up at him from the grass. And when the job had been done again, the Rat pointed out a fork which one of them ought to have seen. Last of all, the mustard-pot, which Mole had been sitting on - and the job was finished!

The afternoon sun was setting low as Rat rowed gently homewards in a dreamy mood, murmuring poetry to himself, and not paying much attention to Mole.

By now the Mole was feeling quite at home in a boat (or so he thought) and was getting a bit restless. "Ratty! Please. I want to row now!"

The Rat shook his head with a smile. "Not yet, my young friend," he said. "Wait till you've had a few lessons. It's not as easy as it looks."

Mole was quiet for a minute or two. But he began to feel more and more jealous of Rat, rowing so strongly and so easily along. A small voice inside him began to whisper that he could do it just as well.

The Mole jumped up and seized the oars so suddenly that the Rat, who was gazing out over the water, was taken by surprise and fell backwards off his seat with his legs in the air. Swiftly, the Mole jumped in his place and grabbed the oars.

"Stop it, you silly fool!" cried the Rat, from the bottom of the boat. "You can't do it! You'll have us over!"

The Mole flung his oars back with a flourish, and made a great big dig at the water. He missed the surface altogether, his legs flew up above his head, and he found himself lying on the top of the poor Rat. Greatly alarmed, he made a grab at the side of the boat, and the next moment - Sploosh! over went the boat, and he found himself struggling in the river.

Oh my, how cold the water was, and oh, how very wet it felt. How it sang in his ears as he went down, down, down! How bright and welcome the sun looked as he rose to the surface coughing and spluttering! How afraid he was when he felt himself sinking again! Then a firm paw gripped him by the back of his neck. It was the Rat, and he was laughing. Mole could feel him laughing, right down his arm and through his paws and into his neck.

The Rat got hold of an oar and shoved it under the Mole's arm; then he did the same by the other side of him and, swimming behind, pushed the poor animal to shore, hauled him out, and set him down on the bank, a squashy, pulpy lump of misery.

When the Rat had rubbed him down a bit, and wrung some of the wet out of him, he said, "Now then, old fellow! Trot up and down on the bank as hard as you can, till you're warm and dry again, while I dive for the picnic-basket."

So the unhappy Mole, wet on the outside and ashamed on the inside, trotted about till he was fairly dry.

Meanwhile, the Rat dived into the water again, brought back the boat and tied her up. Then he dived for the picnic-basket and struggled to land with it.

When all was ready for a start once more, the Mole, sad and ashamed, took his seat in the stern of the boat. As they set off, he said in a trembling voice, "Ratty, my generous friend. I am very sorry indeed for my foolish and ungrateful behaviour. I almost lost that beautiful picnic-basket. I have been a complete fool, and I know it. Will you forgive me, and let things go on as before?"

"That's all right!" said Rat cheerily. "What's a little wet to a Water Rat? Look here, I think you'd better come and stop with me for a little while. I can make you comfortable - and I'll teach you to row, and to swim, and you'll soon be as handy in the water as any of us."

The Mole was so touched by Ratty's kind words that he could find no voice to answer him (and had to brush away a tear or two with the back of his paw).

But the Rat kindly looked away, and very soon the Mole felt happy again.

When they got home, the Rat made a bright fire in the parlour, and placed Mole in an armchair in front of it, having fetched down a dressing-gown and slippers for him.

Then the Rat told Mole river stories till supper time. Very thrilling stories they were too, to a Mole who had lived in a dark burrow all his life. Stories all about weirs and floods, leaping pike and herons. All about adventures down drains and night fishing with Otter.

Supper was a most cheerful
meal, but very shortly afterwards a
terribly sleepy Mole had to be taken
upstairs by the kind Water Rat.

Mole was given the best bedroom, where he soon laid his
head on his pillow quite happily knowing that his new found
friend, the River, was lapping the sill of his window.

This day was only the first of many similar ones for the Mole, and the start of many adventures during the long summer months he spent with the Rat.

He learnt to swim and to row; he learnt to love the water, and when Mole put his ear near the reeds he definitely could hear the wind whispering in the willows.

In this story from
'The Wind in the Willows' the Water Rat
takes his friend Mole to meet Mr. Toad at Toad Hall.
The excited Toad leads them off on an adventure,
which of course ends in disaster!

THE WIND IN THE WILLOWS

The Open Road

"Ratty," said Mole suddenly one bright summer morning, "if you please, I want to ask you a favour. Will you take me to meet Mr. Toad?"

"Why, certainly," said the good natured Rat jumping to his feet. "Get the boat out and we'll paddle up there at once. It's never the wrong time to call on Toad. Early or late he's always the same fellow. Always good tempered, always glad to see you, always sorry when you go."

"He must be a very nice animal," said the Mole, as he got into the boat and took the oars.

"He is the very best of animals," the Rat went on. "So simple, so good natured, and so affectionate. Perhaps he is a bit boastful - but he has got some great qualities has Toady!"

Rounding a bend in the river, they saw a handsome old house built of mellow red brick, with lawns reaching down to the water's edge.

"There's Toad Hall," said the Rat. "Toad is very rich, and this is one of the nicest houses in these parts, though we never admit as much to Toad!"

As they glided up the creek, they passed a large boathouse. It was full of beautiful boats, but not one in the water. The place looked quite forgotten.

The Rat looked around him. "I understand that Toad is fed up with boats now! I wonder what his new craze is? No doubt we shall find out soon enough!"

Mole and Ratty stepped out of their boat and strolled across the lawns in search of Toad. They found him sitting in a wicker garden chair, a large map spread out in front of him.

"Hooray!" he cried jumping up. "This is splendid!" He shook the paws of both animals warmly (he never even asked to be introduced to Mole).

"How kind of you!" he went on, dancing round them. "I was just going to send a boat down the river for you, Ratty, with strict orders for you to be fetched up here at once. Come inside both of you!"

"Let's sit quiet a bit, Toady!" said the Rat, throwing himself into an armchair, while Mole took another by the side of him. "Were you going to ask my advice about rowing?" asked the Rat.

"Oh, pooh! boating!" interrupted Toad in disgust. "What a waste of time - gave that up long ago. No, I've discovered an interest to last me a lifetime!"

A very excited Mr. Toad led the way to the stable yard; and there, drawn out of the coach house and into the open, they saw a gipsy caravan shining and new, painted a canary-yellow picked out with green, and red wheels.

"There you are!" cried Toad, standing before them legs apart, chest out. "There's real life for you. The open road, the dusty highway, villages, towns, cities. Here today and somewhere else tomorrow. Come inside and look. Planned it all myself, I did!"

The Mole was very interested and excited, and followed Toad up the steps and into the caravan. Rat only snorted and thrust his hands deep into his pockets, remaining where he was.

It was indeed very compact and comfortable. Little sleeping bunks - a little table that folded up against the wall - a cooking stove, lockers, bookshelves, a bird cage with a bird in it, and pots, pans, jugs and kettles of every shape and size.

"All complete!" said Toad triumphantly, pulling open a locker. "You see - biscuits, potted lobster, sardines - everything you could possibly want. Soda water here - tobacco there - notepaper, bacon, jam, cards and dominoes. You'll find that nothing whatever has been forgotten, when we make our start this afternoon!"

"I beg your pardon," said Rat slowly. "Did I overhear you say that we make a start this afternoon?"

"Now, you dear, good old Ratty," pleaded Toad, "you must come, I can't possibly manage without you. You can't possibly want to stay on your smelly old river all your life. I want to show you the world!"

"I don't care," said the Rat stubbornly. "I'm not coming, and that's that. I'm going to stay on my smelly old river. And what's more, Mole is too, aren't you, Mole?"

"Of course I am," said Mole loyally. "I'll always stick to you, Ratty. All the same, it sounds as if it might have been fun!"

The Rat could see that his friend Mole would really love to go and he hated to disappoint him.

During lunch, Toad painted such a wonderful picture of life in a caravan, that Mole could hardly sit in his chair for excitement.

Somehow, it soon seemed taken for granted by all three of them that the trip was settled.

Ratty couldn't bear to disappoint his two dear friends and that was the only reason he agreed to go.

When they were quite ready, Toad led Ratty and Mole to the paddock to try to capture the old grey horse who was going to pull the caravan. However, the horse preferred to stay in his paddock - and took a great deal of catching.

At last the horse was harnessed and they set off, all talking at once!

It was a lovely afternoon. They walked along either side of the cart or sat on the shaft, kicking up the dust as they went.

From the orchards by the road, birds whistled to them cheerily. People passing them called "Good day," or stopped to say nice things about their beautiful caravan; and the rabbits, sitting at their front doors in the hedgerows, held up their paws and said, "Oh my! Oh my! Oh my!"

Late in the evening, tired and happy and miles from home, they drew up on a common, far away from any houses or people.

They turned the horse loose to graze, and ate their simple supper sitting on the grass by the side of the caravan. Toad boasted about all he was going to do in the days to come, while the stars came out and a yellow moon appeared as if from nowhere.

At last they turned into their little bunks in the caravan; and Toad, kicking out his legs, sleepily said, "Well, good night, you fellows! This is the real life for a gentleman! Talk about your old river!"

"I don't talk about my river," replied the Rat patiently. "You know I don't, Toad. But I think about it," he added sadly. "I think about it - all the time."

The Mole reached out from under his blanket, felt for the Rat's paw in the darkness and gave it a squeeze. "I'll do whatever you like, Ratty," he whispered. "Shall we run away tomorrow morning, quite early - very early - and go back to our dear old hole on the river?"

"No, no, we'll see it out," whispered back the Rat. "Thanks awfully, but I ought to stick by Toad till this trip is ended. It wouldn't be safe for him to be left to himself. It won't take very long. His fads never do. Good night!"

The end was indeed nearer than even the Rat suspected.

After so much open air and excitement the Toad slept very soundly, and no amount of shaking could get him out of bed next morning. So the Mole and the Rat set to work.

The Rat saw to the horse, and lit a fire, cleaned last night's cups and plates, then got things ready for breakfast.

The Mole trudged off to the nearest village, a long way off, for milk and eggs and everything that Toad had forgotten to provide.

The hard work had all been done, and the two animals were resting, quite tired out, by the time Toad appeared on the scene. He was fresh and bright, remarking about a pleasant easy life they were all leading now, after all the cares and worries of house-keeping at home.

They had a pleasant ramble that day over grassy downs and along narrow lanes. They camped that night, as before, on a grassy common. Only this time Rat and Mole took care that Toad should do his fair share of the work.

Now when the time came for starting next morning, Toad was not so happy about his new easy life. In fact, he tried to get back into his bunk, until Ratty and Mole pulled him out by force.

They went on their way, as before, across country by narrow lanes, and it was not till the afternoon that they came out on to the highway. It was their first highway. It was there that disaster, sudden and unexpected, struck them.

So great was the disaster - that Toad would never be the same again!

They were strolling along the road quite slowly. Mole was by the horse's head, chatting to him (as the poor thing had been feeling a bit left out). Toad and Rat were walking behind the cart talking together. At least Toad was talking and Rat was listening!

When, suddenly from behind them, they heard a faint warning hum, like the drone of a distant bee. Glancing back, they saw a small cloud of dust with a dark centre coming towards them at incredible speed, while from out of the dust a faint "Poop-poop!" could be heard.

Toad and Mole went on talking when, all of a sudden, a blast of wind and a whirl of sound made them jump for the nearest ditch.

The "Poop-poop" rang with a blaring shout in their ears. They had a moment's glimpse of the inside of a magnificent glittering motor car, with its driver hugging tight onto its wheel.

It flung a cloud of dust that blinded and totally covered Toad, Rat and Mole. Then it disappeared to a speck in the distance, sounding like a droning bee once more.

The old grey horse, dreaming, as he plodded along, of his quiet paddock, had never had such a fright! Rearing, plunging, backing steadily (in spite of Mole's efforts to calm him) he drove the cart backwards towards the deep ditch at the side of the road. It wavered an instant - then there was a heart-rending crash - and the canary-coloured cart lay on its side in the ditch, a total wreck!

The Rat danced up and down the road in temper. "You villains!" he shouted, shaking both fists. "You scoundrels, you road-hogs! I'll have the law on you!" His homesickness all forgotten.

Toad sat in the middle of the dusty road, his legs stretched out in front of him, simply staring at the disappearing motor car, with a very strange expression on his face, quietly murmuring, "Poop-poop!"

The Mole was busy trying to quieten the horse, which he managed to do after a time.

Then he went to look at the caravan on its side in the ditch. It was a sorry sight! Panels and windows smashed, axles hopelessly bent, sardine tins scattered all over the wide world and the poor bird in the cage calling to be let out.

The Rat came over to help Mole, but both of them were not strong enough to right the caravan. "Hi! Toad!" they cried. "Come and lend a hand, can't you!"

The Toad never answered a word, or budged from his seat in the road, so they went to see what was the matter with him.

They found him in a sort of dream, a happy smile on his face, his eyes fixed on the cloud of dust left by the speeding motor car. Every so often Rat and Mole heard him murmur, "Poop-poop!"

The Rat shook him by the shoulder. "Are you coming to help us, Toad?" he demanded sternly.

"Glorious, stirring sight!" murmured Toad, never offering to move. "The real way to travel. The only way to travel. Here today - in next week tomorrow. Oh bliss! Oh poop-poop! Oh my! Oh my!"

"Oh stop being a fool, Toad!" cried the Mole in despair.

"And to think I never knew," the Toad went on, "all those wasted years that lie behind me. But now that I know, now that I fully realise. What dust clouds shall spring up behind me as I speed along! What carts shall I fling carelessly into the ditch. Horrid little carts - common carts - canary-coloured carts!"

"What are we to do with him?" asked the Mole of the Water Rat.

"Nothing at all," replied the Rat firmly. "You see I know him of old. He's got a new craze, and it always takes him this way. He'll be like this for days now. Never mind him. Let's go and see what can be done about the caravan."

They inspected the caravan most carefully, it was damaged beyond repair. The axles were in a hopeless state, and the missing wheel was shattered into pieces.

The Rat knotted the horse's reins over his back and took him by the lead, carrying the birdcage in the other hand. "Come on!" he said grimly to Mole. "It's five or six miles to the nearest town, and we shall have to walk it. The sooner we make a start the better!"

"But what about Toad?" asked the Mole anxiously, as they set off together. "We can't leave him here, sitting in the middle of the road by himself, the state he is in. It's not safe. Suppose another motor car were to come along."

"Oh bother Toad," said the Rat angrily, "I've done with him."

They had not gone very far on their way, when there was a pattering of feet behind them, and Toad caught them up and thrust a paw inside the elbow of each of them; still panting and staring into space.

"Now look here, Toad," said the Rat sharply, "as soon as we get to town, you'll have to go straight to the police station. See who owns that motor car and make a complaint about it. And then you'll have to find a blacksmith to mend the caravan. Meanwhile the Mole and I will go to an inn and find comfortable rooms where we can stay until the caravan's ready and till your nerves have got over the shock!"

"Police station!" murmured Toad dreamily. "Me complain about that beautiful, that heavenly motor car. Never!

"As for mending that cart! I've done with carts for ever. I never want to see or hear of it again. Oh, Ratty. Thank you for coming with me on this trip. Without you I might never have seen that wonderful motor car. I owe it all to you, my best of friends!"

The Rat turned from him in despair. "He's quite hopeless. I give up!" he said to Mole. "When we get to town we'll go to the railway station and catch a train that will take us back to the River Bank tonight!"

After a very long tiring walk they finally reached the town. They went straight to the railway station and left Toad in the waiting room, giving a porter two pence to keep a strict eye on him.

Then they left the horse at an inn stable, and left word for the caravan to be mended and returned to Toad.

Eventually, a slow train took them to a station not very far from Toad Hall.

The Rat and the Mole helped the spellbound, sleep-walking Toad to his door, put him inside, and asked his housekeeper to feed him and see he got to bed.

Then they got their boat from the boathouse, rowed down the river, and at a very late hour sat down to supper in their own snug little riverside parlour, to the Rat's great joy and contentment.

The following evening the Mole, who had got up late and taken things very easy all day, was sitting on the bank fishing, when the Rat, who had been looking up his friends and gossiping, came strolling along to find him.

"Heard the news?" he said. "There's nothing else being talked about, all along the river bank. Toad went up to town by an early train this morning. And he has ordered a large and very expensive motor car."

But that will be another story...

It had been a fine spring day when the Water Rat had taken
Mole for his first row on the river.
The Rat had packed a luncheon basket full of the
most delicious food.
As they began their picnic two of Rat's friends appeared.
One was Otter, who came out of the water to join them.
The other was Mr. Badger who popped out from behind a tree,
grunted, and disappeared!
Ever since that day, Mole longed to meet the mysterious Mr.
Badger again.
In this story he sets off alone to find him....

THE WIND IN THE WILLOWS

The Wild Wood

The Mole had long wanted to meet Mr. Badger. He seemed such an important fellow. Everyone knew of him but hardly ever saw him.

"Badger will turn up some day or another, and then I'll introduce you!" promised the Rat.

"Couldn't you ask him here to dinner or something?" said the Mole.

"He wouldn't come," replied the Rat simply. "Badger hates coming to dinner, and all that sort of thing."

"Well, then, supposing we go and call on him?" suggested the Mole.

"Oh, I'm sure he wouldn't like that at all!" said the Rat, quite alarmed. "Besides, we can't, because he lives in the very middle of the Wild Wood! He'll come here some day, if you wait long enough."

But Badger never did come. The summer was long over and winter was on its way. Mole waited and waited, still longing to meet this mysterious grey Badger who lived by himself in the middle of the Wild Wood.

So it was, that on one winter's day, when the Mole had a good deal of spare time on his hands, that he decided to go out by himself and explore the Wild Wood - and perhaps meet Mr. Badger.

The Rat was dozing in his armchair in front of a blazing fire when Mole slipped quietly out of the warm parlour and into the open air.

The afternoon sky was cold and grey and the countryside bare and leafless. Mole had never been so far before and he was beginning to quite enjoy the different look of the fields and trees in winter.

In fact he felt very cheerful as he pushed on towards the Wild Wood, which lay before him low and threatening.

There was nothing to frighten him at first. Twigs crackled under his feet, logs tripped him, fungi on stumps looked like faces and startled him for a moment; but that was all fun and exciting. It led him on, and he went deeper into the wood where the light was less and the trees made ugly frightening shapes.

Everything was very still now. Dusk was falling and, little by little, the light was fading.

Then the faces began. First a little evil wedge-shaped face, looking out at him from a hole - then vanishing.

He quickened his pace, telling himself cheerfully not to begin imagining things!

Then suddenly, Mole seemed to see a face in every hole; hundreds of them staring at him with evil hard eyes. Quickly he dived off the path and plunged deep into the wood itself.

Then the whistling began. Very faint and shrill it was, and far behind him - the Mole hurried forward - and there it was again - in front of him this time. Poor Mole was quite alone, far from help and the night was closing in.

Then the pattering began. He thought it was only falling leaves at first! But no! It seemed to be the pat-pat-pat of little feet. Was it in front or behind?

As he stood still to listen, a rabbit came running hard towards him, "Get out of this, you fool, get out!" the Mole heard him mutter as he swung round a stump and disappeared down a friendly burrow.

The pattering increased. The whole wood seemed to be running now and closing in around poor Mole.

In panic, he began to run too. He bumped into things, fell over things and darted under things. At last he hid in the deep, dark hollow of an old beech tree.

As he lay there panting and trembling and listening to the whistlings and patterings outside he knew, at last, the thing that Ratty had tried to keep him away from: the Terror of the Wild Wood!

Meanwhile, the Rat, warm and comfortable, dozed by his fireside. Then a coal slipped, the fire crackled and sent up a spurt of flame and he awoke with a start.

He looked round for Mole, but Mole was not there! He listened for a while. The house seemed very quiet.

Then he called "Moley!" several times, and, getting no answer, got up and went into the hall.

The Mole's cap was missing from its peg, and his galoshes were also gone.

Rat left the house and found Mole's footprints outside in the mud leading straight to the Wild Wood.

The Rat looked very grave. Then he went back into his house, strapped a belt round his waist, shoved a pair of pistols into it, took a stout stick, and set off for the Wild Wood at a smart pace!

It was already getting dark when he reached the first fringe of trees. Straight away he rushed deep into the wood looking for any sign of the Mole.

Here and there wicked little faces popped out of holes, but vanished at the sight of the brave Water Rat. The whistling and pattering died away, and all was very still.

The Rat made his way through the dark wood, all the time calling out cheerfully, "Moley! Moley! Moley! Where are you? It's me - it's old Rat!"

Then at last to his joy, he heard a little answering cry. From out of a hole in an old beech tree came a feeble voice saying, "Ratty, is that really you?"

The Rat crept into the hollow and there he found the Mole, exhausted and still trembling. "Oh, Rat!" he cried, "I've been so frightened, you can't think!"

The Mole was greatly cheered up by the sight of the Rat's stick and his gleaming pistols, and he stopped shivering and began to feel bolder and more himself again.

"Now then," said the Rat presently, "we really must start for home while there's still a little light left. It would never do to spend the night here!"

"Dear Ratty," said the poor Mole, "I'm simply dead beat. You must let me rest a while and get my strength back."

"Oh, alright," said the good-natured Rat, "rest away, it's nearly pitch dark now anyhow, and there ought to be a bit of moon later."

So the Mole stretched himself out on the dry leaves and went to sleep while the Rat lay patiently waiting, with a pistol in his paw.

When at last the Mole woke up, the Rat said, "I'll take a look outside, then we really must be off."

The Rat went to the entrance of their hollow tree. Then the Mole heard him say quietly to himself, "Hello! Hello! Well I never!"

"What's up, Ratty?" asked the Mole.

"Snow is up," replied the Rat briefly, "or rather, down! It's snowing hard."

A gleaming carpet of snow was springing up everywhere, filling the air with its fine, delicate powder.

"We must make a start," said the Rat. "The worst of it is, I don't know exactly where we are and this snow makes everything look so different."

It did indeed! However they set out bravely, trying to find the right path.

An hour or two later, they had lost all track of time - they pulled up, downhearted, weary and hopelessly lost!

They were aching and bruised with tumbles; they had fallen into several holes and got wet through. The snow was getting so deep that they could hardly drag their little legs through it.

"We can't sit here very long," said the Rat. "We must try to find a cave or a hole with a dry floor, out of the wind and the snow!"

So, once more they got to their feet and struggled on through the whirling snow, when, suddenly, Mole tripped up and fell forward on his face with a groan. "Oh, my leg," he cried. "Oh, my poor shin!" and he sat up on the snow and nursed his leg in both front paws. "I must have tripped over a hidden branch or a stump," went on the Mole miserably.

"That was never done by a branch or stump," said Ratty examining the Mole's leg. "Looks as if it was made by a sharp metal edge. Funny!"

"It hurts just the same, whatever done it!" cried poor Mole as the Rat carefully tied up the leg with his handkerchief.

Then to Mole's surprise, the Rat began to scratch and shovel the snow. Suddenly, the Rat cried, "Hooray! Hooray!" and danced a jig in the snow. "Come and see what I've found!"

The Mole hobbled up to the spot and had a good look; just peeping above the snow was a door-scraper!

The Rat set to work once more, digging down deep in the snow he discovered - a doormat!

Quick as he could Rat attacked the snow bank beside them with his stick, and Mole scraped busily away too.

After ten minutes of hard work the point of Rat's stick struck something that sounded hollow. Faster and harder they dug, until, in full view of the astonished Mole, a solid looking door appeared.

It was painted dark green. An iron bell pull hung by the side, and below it, on a small brass plate, neatly written, they could read by the aid of moonlight:

'MR. BADGER.'

The Mole fell backwards on the snow from sheer surprise and delight. "Rat!" he cried, "you're a real wonder, that's what you are!"

"Get up at once and hang on to that bell pull," ordered the Rat. "Ring as hard as you can, while I hammer."

While the Rat attacked the door with his stick, the Mole sprang up at the bell pull, clutched it and swung there, both feet off the ground, and from quite a long way off they could faintly hear a deep toned bell respond.

They waited patiently for what seemed to be a very long time, stamping in the snow to keep their feet warm. At last they heard the sound of slow shuffling footsteps approaching the door from inside.

There was the noise of a bolt shooting back and the door opened a few inches, enough to show a long snout and a pair of sleepy, blinking eyes.

"Now, who is it this time, disturbing people on such a night?" said a gruff voice.

"Oh, Badger," cried the Rat, "let us in, please. It's me, Rat, and my friend Mole, and we've lost our way in the snow."

"What, Ratty, my dear little man!" exclaimed the Badger, in quite a different voice. "Come in, both of you. You must be frozen. Well I never! Lost in the snow! And in the Wild Wood too, and at this time of night!"

The Badger, who wore a long dressing gown and slippers, had probably been on his way to bed when he heard their call.

He looked down at them kindly and patted both their heads. "This is not the sort of night for small animals to be out," he said. "Come along into the kitchen, there's a first rate fire there, and supper and everything."

He shuffled on in front of them, carrying the light, and they followed him, nudging each other in an excited sort of way, down a long gloomy passage, until they came to several stout doors. One of which Badger flung open, and at once they found themselves in all the glow and warmth of a fire lit kitchen.

The floor was well worn red brick, and on the wide hearth burnt a fire of logs with a couple of high backed seats on either side.

In the middle of the room stood a long table with benches down each side. Rows of spotless plates winked from the shelves of the dresser, and, from the rafters overhead, hung hams, bundles of dried herbs, nets of onions and baskets of eggs.

The kindly Badger sat them down on seats to toast themselves at the fire and made them remove their wet coats and boots. Then he fetched them dressing gowns and slippers, and bathed Mole's shin with warm water.

Warm and dry at last, it seemed that the Wild Wood they had just left outside was miles and miles away.

When at last, they were thoroughly toasted, the Badger called them to the table where he had been busy laying a meal.

He sat in his armchair at the head of the table as they ate their supper. Then he listened as Ratty and Mole told of their adventures that night in the Wild Wood, and soon Mole began to feel that Badger was quite a friendly type really!

When supper was finished they chatted a while, sitting together in the firelight.

Although it was getting rather late, the Mole felt quite lively and wide awake, but the poor, tired Water Rat was worn out and kept nodding off in the Badger's warm kitchen.

"It's time we were all in bed," said Badger, getting up and fetching candlesticks. "Take your time getting up tomorrow morning - breakfast at any hour you please!"

He led the animals to a long room that seemed half bedroom and half loft. The Badger's winter stores were everywhere. They took up half the room: piles of apples, turnips, potatoes, baskets full of nuts, and jars of honey. But two little beds on the remainder of the floor looked soft and inviting, and the bed linen on them was clean and smelt of lavender. The Mole and the Water Rat shook off their clothes and tumbled in between the sheets with great joy and contentment.

When the two tired animals came down to breakfast very late next morning, they found two young hedgehogs sitting on a bench at the table, eating porridge out of wooden bowls.

"Where have you youngsters come from? Lost your way in the snow, I suppose?" the Rat asked pleasantly.

"Yes, please, sir," said the elder of the two hedgehogs respectfully. "Me and little Billy was trying to find our way to school, and Billy got frightened and cried. And at last we came and knocked on Mr. Badger's back door. For everyone knows he's such a kind hearted gentleman!"

"I understand," said Rat, cutting himself some rashers from a side of bacon, while Mole dropped some eggs into a pan. "What's the weather like outside?"

"Oh, terrible bad, sir, terrible deep the snow is!" said the hedgehog.

Suddenly the front door bell clanged loudly, and the Rat, who was very greasy with buttered toast, sent Billy, the smaller hedgehog, to see who it might be.

There was the sound of much stamping in the hall and Billy returned with the Otter, who was delighted to see Ratty and Mole safe and sound.

"Thought I'd find you here alright," said the Otter cheerfully. "Everyone on the River Bank was very worried about you both," the Otter went on. "Ratty never been home all night - nor Mole either - something dreadful must have happened, they said, and the snow had covered up all your tracks. So I came straight here to Badger's house, through the Wild Wood and the snow. My! It was fine coming through the snow, every now and then masses of snow slid off the branches, making me jump and run for cover. Snow castles and snow caverns had sprung up over night - I could have stayed and played with them for hours. Then I met a rabbit sitting on a stump. He was such a silly fellow, I had to cuff him round the ears to get any sense out of him. The rabbits in the Wild Wood knew very well that you were lost and Mole was hurt - why didn't they do something to help?"

"Weren't you at all - er - nervous?" asked the Mole remembering yesterday's terror in the Wild Wood.

"Nervous?" The Otter showed a gleaming set of strong, white teeth as he laughed. "I'd give 'em nerves if any of them tried anything on with me. Here, Mole, fry me some slices of ham. I'm terribly hungry, and I've got a lot to say to Ratty, haven't seen him for ages!"

So Mole cut some slices of ham and told the hedgehogs to fry it, and returned to his own breakfast.

Badger, who had been asleep in his study, was pleased to see the Otter and invited him to lunch.

"Here, you two youngsters, be off home to your mother!" said Badger kindly to the two young hedgehogs, as he gave them sixpence each and patted their heads, and sent someone to show them the way.

All during that morning the four friends talked and talked. Then they sat down to lunch together, and afterwards they talked some more!

The Otter and the Rat settled down to talk about their beloved River Bank while Badger lit a lantern and took Mole on a tour down the dim passages of his underground home.

Now Mole was naturally an underground animal by birth, and Badger's house suited him exactly, and made him feel at home - but not the Water Rat!

When they got back to the kitchen they found him walking up and down, very restless, longing to get back to his River Bank.

So he had his overcoat on, and his pistols thrust into his belt again. "Come along, Mole," he said, as soon as he caught a sight of them. "We must get off while it's daylight. Don't want to spend another night in the Wild Wood again."

"You really needn't fret, Ratty," said the Badger. "My passages run further than you think. In fact some of them run beneath the wood, right to the very edge."

The Rat was so eager to be off, that Badger took his lantern and led the way through a maze of tunnels, until, at last, daylight began to show itself through the mouth of the passage.

Badger bade the three friends a hasty goodbye and pushed them through the opening.

They found themselves standing on the very edge of the Wild Wood. Rocks and brambles and tree-roots behind them; in front a great space of quiet fields and, far ahead, a glint of the old familiar river.

The Otter, knowing all the paths, took charge of the party, and they trailed out on a bee-line for a distant stile.

Looking back, they saw the Wild Wood, dark and menacing, behind them.

Together they turned and made for home, for firelight, and for the voice of the River that they knew and trusted, sounding cheerily outside their window.

Here are some of the exciting
adventures of Mr. Toad, who is very rich and lives in a huge
mansion called Toad Hall.
Now Toad is really a very nice fellow, but rather boastful and
inclined to show off. He can't resist trying anything new, his
latest craze is motor cars!
When his friends, Ratty and Mole, hear how this new craze is
getting Toad into trouble with the police, they decide to try and
do something about it....

THE WIND IN THE WILLOWS

The Adventures of Mr. Toad

It was a bright morning in the early part of summer and the Mole and the Water Rat had been up since dawn, very busy getting ready for the boating season.

They were finishing breakfast in their little parlour and eagerly discussing their plans for the day, when a heavy knock sounded at the door.

"Bother!" said the Rat, egg all over him. "See who it is, Mole, like a good fellow, since you've finished."

The Mole went to answer the door, and Rat heard him utter a cry of surprise, "It's Mr. Badger!"

Now Badger never ever called to see anyone - so this must be a call of some importance.

The Badger strode heavily into the room looking very serious. The Rat let his egg spoon fall on the table cloth and sat open-mouthed.

"The hour has come!" said the Badger, "to do something about Toad! I learned last night," he continued, "that another new and very powerful motor car will arrive at Toad Hall today."

Now all three friends had to agree that they simply must put a stop to Toad's hopelessly bad driving. They had lost count of the cars he had crashed and the fines he had paid.

"He'll be ruined or killed or both," said Ratty. "Badger! We are his friends, we ought to do something!"

So they set off up the road to Toad Hall, to find as the Badger had expected, a shiny new motor car of great size - painted a bright red - standing in front of the house.

As they neared the door it was flung open, and Mr. Toad, dressed in goggles, cap, gaiters and enormous overcoat, came swaggering down the steps, pulling on his gloves.

The Badger strode up the steps. "Take him inside," he said sternly to Rat and Mole. Then, as Toad was hustled through the door, struggling and protesting, Badger turned to the chauffeur in charge of the new motor car.

"I'm afraid you won't be wanted today," he said. "Mr. Toad has changed his mind. He will not require the car!"

"Now then!" he said to Toad, when the four of them stood together in the hall, "first of all take those ridiculous things off!"

"Shan't!" replied Toad with great spirit.

"Take them off him, then, you two," ordered the Badger briefly.

Toad kicked and yelled and called them all sorts of names. The Rat sat on him, and Mole got his motor-clothes off him bit by bit, and they stood him up on his legs again.

"You knew it must come to this, sooner or later, Toad," the Badger explained severely. "You're getting us a bad name by your furious driving and your smashes and your rows with the police."

Then Badger took Toad into another room and gave him a real talking-to. After almost an hour he came out with a very sorry looking Toad.

"My friends," said Badger, "I'm pleased to tell you that Toad is truly sorry for his bad behaviour, and has promised to give up motor cars for ever."

There was a long pause. Toad looked this way and that. At last he spoke, "I am not sorry. Motor cars are simply wonderful! In fact, I promise that the very first one I see, off I shall go in it!"

"Very well then," said Badger firmly. "We shall lock you upstairs in your room until this silly craze for motor cars is over!"

So poor Toad, kicking and struggling, was hauled upstairs by his three faithful friends.

As Mole turned the key on him and went downstairs, Toad shouted abuse through the keyhole.

"I've never seen Toad so determined," said Badger. "He must never be left for an instant, until he has forgotten all about those stupid motor cars!"

They arranged to keep watch over him. Each animal took it in turns to sleep in Toad's room, and they divided up the day between them.

One fine morning, it was Rat's turn to be on duty. He found Toad still in bed saying he was far too ill to get up.

"Go to the village and fetch the doctor, Ratty!" murmured Toad feebly, "before it's too late!"

The Water Rat was very alarmed and hurried from the room, locked the door behind him and ran off to the village.

The Toad, who had hopped lightly out of bed as soon as he heard the key turn in the lock, watched him eagerly from the window till he disappeared down the drive.

Then, laughing heartily, he dressed as quickly as possible, and, knotting the sheets from his bed together, he scrambled out of the window and slid to the ground. And, taking the opposite direction to Rat, marched off light-heartedly, whistling a merry tune.

How gloomy the three friends felt, when Rat admitted to Mole and Badger just how easily he had been taken in by Toad.

How conceited Toad looked as he strode along, his head in the air, thinking to himself how clever he was outsmarting poor old Ratty!

Soon he was miles away from Toad Hall, and beginning to feel very hungry. He stopped at the first inn he found and ordered the best meal they had.

Toad was halfway through his meal when he heard a familiar sound that made him jump and tremble all over.

A motor car turned into the yard and came to a stop. The driver got out and called into the inn for a meal. All of a sudden, Toad had a splendid idea! He paid his bill, slipped quietly out of the inn, and went straight round to the yard. "There can't be any harm in just looking at it!"

The car stood in the middle of the yard. No one was there! Toad walked slowly around it. "I wonder if this sort of car starts easily?"

Next moment, hardly knowing how it happened, he had turned the starting handle and jumped into the driver's seat. As if in a dream, he swung the car round the yard and drove off through the archway.

Soon he was speeding along the highway and out into the open country. Faster and faster Toad went, not knowing where he was going, nor caring what might happen to him.

Sad to say the worst did happen! Toad found himself in court. There he was standing trembling all alone in the dock, a policeman either side of him. Poor Toad! No one to help him get out of this mess, and his dear friends, Ratty, Mole and Badger, miles away.

The court found Toad guilty of stealing a valuable motor car, dangerous driving and being rude to the police. Worse was to come! They sent Toad to prison for twenty years!

The poor fellow was handcuffed to two policemen and dragged, shrieking and screaming, across the market-place into a grim old castle, which was to be his prison.

Toad was taken down the steps to the deepest dungeon they could find.

"Guard this villainous criminal with your life!" one of the policemen ordered the old gaoler who was put in charge of Toad.

The gaoler nodded as he put Toad inside his cell. The rusty key turned in the lock, the great door clanged behind him, and Toad was a helpless prisoner.

Alone and locked away in a damp and dark dungeon, Toad flung himself on the floor and shed bitter tears of despair.

"This is the end of everything," cried the unhappy Toad. "This is the end of the career of Toad, the popular, handsome Toad, the rich and hospitable Toad! How can I ever hope to be free again? Oh, unhappy and forsaken Toad!"

He was so miserable, he cried all day and all night. He refused all the meals the gaoler brought to him, he was so busy feeling sorry for himself.

Now the gaoler had a pretty and kind-hearted daughter who was very fond of animals. Because she couldn't bear seeing Toad so unhappy, she begged her father to let her look after the poor animal.

"Now, cheer up, Toad," she said as she unlocked his cell. "Sit up and dry your eyes and be a sensible animal. And do try to eat a bit of dinner!"

But Toad still wailed, kicked his legs and refused to be comforted.

So the wise girl went away, but she left the plate of hot food, which to the hungry Toad, smelt very appetising. Between mouthfuls and sniffs and sobs, Toad began to cheer up - just a little!

When the girl came back a few hours later, she carried a tray with fresh tea and a plate of hot, buttered toast.

Toad sat up, dried his eyes, sipped his tea and munched his toast, and pretty soon began to boast about himself, his grand house and how important he was!

He told the gaoler's daughter all about Toad Hall and about his friends, Ratty, Mole and Badger, and all of the fun they had together at home.

The girl and Toad had many interesting talks together, as the dreary days went on, the girl grew very sorry for Toad. She hated seeing a poor little animal being locked up at all, for what seemed to her to be a very small crime.

"Toad," said the gaoler's daughter, one morning. "I have an aunt who is a washerwoman. She does washing for all the prisoners in this castle, and she will be coming here tomorrow to return this week's washing."

The girl took a long look at Toad. "You look quite like her - especially your figure! If she would let you have her dress and bonnet, you could escape dressed as a washerwoman!"

At first Toad felt quite offended. "We're not a bit alike, I have a very elegant figure - for a Toad! And another thing," went on Toad, "the great Toad of Toad Hall cannot go about the countryside dressed as a common washerwoman!"

"Then you can stop in prison, you ungrateful Toad!" replied the girl.

At once Toad felt sorry he had sounded so rude. "You are a good, kind, clever girl," he said, "and I am a proud and stupid Toad. Please introduce me to your aunt, so that she might help me."

The very next evening the girl took her aunt to Toad's cell. Inside the bundle of washing she had carefully hidden a cotton gown, an apron, a shawl and a black bonnet.

First they tied the old lady up - just so no one would think that she helped Toad to escape. Quickly, Toad took off his coat and waistcoat and put on the gown and shawl. The gaoler's daughter shook with laughter as she tied the strings of the black bonnet under Toad's chin.

"Now, goodbye, Toad, and good luck - be careful going past the guards!"

With a quaking heart Toad set off. It all seemed so easy.
Not one sentry stopped him! He looked so much like the
washerwoman that every guard let him pass.

At last he heard the great prison door clang shut behind
him, he felt the fresh air on his face and knew that he was free!

Dizzy with the success of his daring escape, he walked
quickly towards the nearest town.

As he went along he heard the
sound of the puffing and snorting of
engines. "This is a piece of luck,"
thought Toad, "a railway station!"

He looked at the timetable, and
found, to his delight, that a train was
going very near Toad hall in half-an-
hour. So off he went to the booking
office to buy his ticket.

He felt in his pocket for the money, when, to his horror, he remembered he had left his waistcoat and jacket and all his money in the prison cell.

"Look here!" said Toad rather grandly, to the man in the ticket office. "I have left my purse behind. Give me a ticket and I will send the money to you!"

"Indeed you will not," snapped the man. "Get away from the window, you are blocking the other passengers!"

Full of despair, Toad wandered blindly down the platform to where the train was standing, tears trickled down each side of his nose.

Very soon his escape would be discovered, the prison guards would hunt him down, they would drag him back again and feed him on bread and water!

Suddenly, Toad found himself opposite the engine, which was being oiled and cleaned by its driver.

"Hello there!" said the man, "what's the trouble?"

"Oh, sir!" said Toad, crying again. "I am a poor washerwoman, I've lost all my money, and can't pay for my ticket. I must get home at once to my poor innocent children," sobbed Toad.

"I'll tell you what," said the engine driver. "My shirts get awful dirty on this engine. If you promise to wash me a few when you get home, you can ride up on the engine!"

Toad's misery turned to rapture, although he had never washed a shirt in his life, and didn't intend to!

The guard waved the flag, the whistle blew, and the train moved out of the station. As the speed increased, Toad thought how every minute was bringing him nearer Toad Hall. He was so happy, he began to skip up and down and sing.

They had travelled many a mile, when Toad noticed a puzzled expression on the engine driver's face. "I could swear there was another train behind us!"

Toad stopped his singing at once and began to feel afraid.

By now the moon was shining brightly and the driver could see quite clearly that they were being followed. "They're gaining on us fast!" cried the engine driver. "It's full of policemen with truncheons and detectives waving revolvers and walking sticks; all waving and shouting the same thing - 'Stop! Stop! Stop!'"

Then Toad fell on his knees among the coals. "Save me, save me, dear, kind Mr. Engine Driver," he pleaded. "I will confess everything! I am not the simple washerwoman I seem to be! I have no children waiting for me. I am the well known and popular Mr. Toad; I have just escaped, by great daring and cleverness, from a grim and dark prison cell. If those fellows on that engine recapture me, they will fling me straight back in there!"

The engine driver looked very grave and said, "I fear that you have been a very wicked Toad and, by rights, I ought to give you up. But as you are in trouble and distress I will not desert you."

Toad felt very relieved.

"I don't like motor cars very much," the driver went on, "and I don't like being ordered about by policemen when I'm on my own engine. So cheer up, Toad! I'll do my best, and we may beat them yet!"

They piled on more coals, shovelling furiously, the furnace roared, the sparks flew, the engine leapt and swung, but still the other engine slowly gained on them.

"It's no good, Toad!" sighed the driver, as he wiped his brow with a rag. "They have the better engine. There's just one thing left to do, so listen carefully to what I tell you. Straight ahead is a long tunnel with a thick wood at the end of it. Now I will put on speed as we are running through the tunnel (the other train will slow down for fear of an accident). When we are through, I will put on the brakes as hard as I can - then you must jump off and hide in the wood. Then I will go full speed ahead again, and they can chase me for as long as they like and as far as they like."

They piled on more coals and the train shot into the tunnel, once they were through the driver shut off steam and put on the brakes.

Toad got down on the step, and as the train slowed down almost to walking pace, he heard the driver call out, "now jump!"

Toad jumped, rolled down a short bank, picked himself up unhurt, scrambled into the wood and hid.

Peeping out, he saw his train pick up speed again and disappear at a great pace.

Then out of the tunnel burst the other engine, roaring and whistling, the policemen and guards waving their weapons and shouting, "Stop! Stop! Stop!"

When they were past, Toad had a good laugh, but he soon stopped when he realised how very late and dark and cold it was. There was he, in an unknown wood, far away from friends and home.

That night, a tired and hungry Toad slept in a hollow tree. However, he managed to make himself comfortable and slept soundly till the morning.

He was awakened at first light by a shaft of bright warm sunlight.

Sitting up, he rubbed his eyes, wondering for a moment where he was. "Oh, joy!" cried Toad, when he remembered he was no longer in prison - he was free!

But all Toad wanted, on that early summer's morning, was to get back to Toad Hall and his dear friends, Ratty, Mole and Badger.

Of course, before he gets home, the great Mr. Toad has many further adventures!

*Ratty carries his wicker
picnic basket.*

*Badger comes to his door
in the Wild Wood.*

*The work was all done by the
time Toad appeared.*

*Ratty sets off for
the river bank.*